D0725407

1918

JOE ALLEN

BALBOA.PRESS
A DIVISION OF HAY HOUSE

This is a work of fiction. All of the characters, names, incidents, organizations, and dialogue in this novel are either the products of the author's imagination or are used fictitiously.

Balboa Press books may be ordered through booksellers or by contacting:

Balboa Press
A Division of Hay House
1663 Liberty Drive
Bloomington, IN 47403
www.balboapress.com
1 (877) 407-4847

Print information available on the last page.

ISBN: 978-1-9822-5097-3 (sc)
ISBN: 978-1-9822-5098-0 (e)

Balboa Press rev. date: 07/15/2020

CONTENTS

INTRODUCTION

"Those who cannot remember the past are condemned to repeat it" This is one of my favorite quotes, attributed to George Santayana. There have been many versions of this quote. Most are descriptions of how we have doomed ourselves by not learning something from our past.

While true to an extent, we can learn a great deal about who we are by learning about our past. In some cases, we could even make some fairly accurate assumptions about our own futures. Using a formulaic approach to revolutions, one may even have been able to predict the complete unfolding of the Arab Spring of recent history: revolution, reaction, the subsequent overreaction, the death and destruction and uncertainty, and hopefully the resolution which may be a long time in coming.

A good history lesson can be as simple as a story. It can also be a series of stories. Every good story needs to be told, and history needs to live on in our future. The desire to be entertained should not be left to just gaming and watching short videos, but in learning about human history through stories told about our past.

A proper, well-rounded education should always involve learning about history and making an effort to understand why things happened the way they did. The focus of a modern education should never be without a good foundation in history.

Of course, we have forgotten more than we can possibly remember, which is why I enjoy filling in some of those blank spots with some elements of human interaction that could have occurred. While learning about history, we can make it more of a set of stories about human existence, rather than the simple memorization of facts. The facts are important, but not the only thing we need to know. A modern education in history should begin with factual-base evidence and an understanding of why things happened the way they did. If we can paint a picture of a person and tell his or her story, the facts begin to make more sense to us today.

The total picture of who we are now is only made complete by the knowledge of our own history. We cannot escape it, so we may as well embrace it. It does not define us in our entirety, nor does it give us no escape for our future. Naturally, we follow our own paths, as the main character in this book will learn.

The true picture of history is not simply defined by the sins of our past, either. The true evaluation of a human is godly, and not something we are qualified to do. We must remember we all have faults, after all, it is the basic failings of humanity. But that is what makes our history so much more fascinating. Those who made history in the past did so with all of their sins and blemishes attached. They made contributions to humanity despite their limitations, and for that we should honor them by learning their stories. This is why I choose to teach and write about history.

PROLOGUE

As I moved to Pennsylvania about 25 years ago, I came to discover, as the birthplace of my parents, that it was "God's Country", to quote my father. The rolling green hills, the lush countryside, and the fertile farmland. I found myself in Berks County, about an hour outside of Philadelphia.

Berks County today has been beaten down by much economically depressive times. There are plenty of reasons for this, naturally. The key indicators to me have been the gradual decline of its county seat, Reading.

At one point, Reading was a bustling town, a small city on its own, not the flyover spot it now seems to be. The school district was at one time, the one after which all schools in the county modelled themselves. The town actually had vacation areas, resorts, even. Dotting the hills around Reading were some unique architectural spots, some resorts, some houses. The town boasted several newspapers, breweries, manufacturing, and even a professional baseball team. You may recall the Monopoly board with the Reading Railroad cards: This could not have been made up from nothing! Reading had a glorious history. Indeed, Reading had its glory days that now seem to have largely passed it by.

As I have learned more about the big town nearest where I live, I am convinced it might one day thrive again. But to understand where it can go, it is important to learn what it once was. To do that is to tell the story of its history.

In this work, you will see a small village, which could be any number of small villages outside of Reading. The town itself still bustles with population, but not like it did a century ago. You will see how it was exciting and full of possibility. All the while, you will also see how the main character is aware of Reading's vibrant history.

The boy could be anyone. I purposefully avoided giving him a name so that one might imagine the name to be a more familiar one, perhaps one's own name. The tone is most closely matched to that of a teenager, something I have learned in a quarter century of teaching.

It is important to point out that the history in this story is a sample of what life was mostly like around the time period of 1918. It is not entirely fiction, nor is it completely non-fiction. The research of the history goes well beyond source citations, but represents years of first-hand learning and instruction. The stories are mostly just made up from elements of my own life, as well as out of my own imagination.

I hope you will find it at the same time inspirational and entertaining as we grapple with our own pandemic of modern times. As any study of history tells us, life goes on. Please enjoy this story, and remember, things will get better!

1918 - CHAPTER ONE

"Do me a favor and be quiet, please!"

How was that fair? I had just about opened my mouth when he just yelled at me. It wasn't like I was the one who started the whole thing. But, one could become easily confused at these times. After all, the whole world seemed to be coming apart. I suppose some more background information would help…

It all started in spring, 1918, two weeks before my birthday. I was excited to be finally turning 18. It would have been nice to enjoy a birthday without the threat of going to war, but that would have to be later, as it turned out.

School was nearing an end, and most of us were not terribly excited by anything our teachers were saying any more. Not that we hated school, it just seemed like the end of it brought about a sort of melancholy: we wanted to move on with our lives, yet we hated the idea of being separated.

My classes were not terribly boring, either. My teachers were very nice, caring people. Some of them seemed passionate and smart, although a few of them just seemed to be waiting out the end as many students were. I just did not see why we needed to finish out the year. No, I could not see a purpose to it. In only three weeks, I would miss that time quite a bit.

Word of the treaty in the war in Europe was getting a lot of attention in the daily newspapers. Seems the Russians were the only thing on the minds of reporters at the time. They totally missed the other evils that would follow. Unfortunately, we would not miss them here.

I was just going about my daily routines, walking to school and taking the scenic route home with my friends when everything started to change. It would all change. Forever.

"Jeremy, get your arm off of me!" shouted Clarisse. I was shocked to hear the two lovebirds fighting. But, as all things seem to come to an end, I suppose this was inevitable.

"Why, what did I do?" was the response. Clarisse just glared at him until he just about shriveled up into his overcoat. It was unseasonably warm that day, but he still had his coat on, and took full advantage of the high collar just then.

It was clear that this was the end of the happy couple. Some thought they would get married, but I did not have that opinion. It was just about the only thing I knew was coming. They always seemed to be bickering, and arguing about one thing or another. Their parents did not like each other, from what I could tell, so I did not think it would last forever. Clarisse confided in me that she noticed him looking at other girls, so Jeremy's trying to pretend he wasn't doing that was pointless. When he put his arm around her, it became a real flashpoint, and she just lost it. She had had enough of that and was ready to move on. He followed along behind us, sulking, at a very slow pace.

There were maybe six of us in that group, like always: me, the former couple, Jimmy Granite, Alan, and his younger sister, Eunice. Eunice and Clarisse walked together, speaking in hushed tones, like they were sharing some kind of secret, and walking just ahead of everyone now, when an old, beat-up buggy clip-clopped up to the edge of the road and the driver, stopping us cold yelled over to us.

"Jimmy, come quick! It's your dad! Something's...happened"

The hesitation was for only a second or two, as we all looked at Jimmy Granite, wondering what he would say about this. He was always making excuses about his dad. Usually, it was to explain why his work was not done in school, that his father did something to it, or made him not complete it. He would tell us his Dad had trouble sleeping, which seemed to be his explanation for just about everything his father did. It seemed like another opportunity to use that excuse again. But he simply looked at us, with a confused expression, taking in our confused-looking faces before he took off toward the buggy. Little did I realize at the time, we would never see Jimmy Granite again.

When I got home, my mother was in the kitchen, getting dinner ready, and father was chopping wood for the evening fire. Nothing seemed out of the ordinary.

I opened my school bag and spread it all out on the kitchen table, ready to begin my work. Honestly, I could not say how long I was at it, when my father came in and had me set it all aside, beginning my chores, clearing the table, and cleaning up around the house. It was not too much work, but I always felt myself complaining. I would never say anything to them, of course. Not sure why, exactly, just knew it was wrong to complain to them.

When my mother had gotten the food together, and we were just about ready for dinner, father and I had washed up and sat down to eat. We said our prayers together and the food was served. Nothing seemed different until the conversation began.

"Tell us about your math lessons today," mother asked. She was not really interested in mathematics, just how I was learning and getting along in school. It was our daily dance. I would explain a lesson our teachers gave and they would act like they understood everything. Seemed a little silly, but at least they made the effort to understand what was going on with me.

"When Mrs. Stefanelli asked us about our math homework, Jimmy Granite gave his typical response: 'I dunno what happened to it, my dad must have ripped it up.' He just keeps blaming his father for everything."

Mother and Father just looked at each other in between bites of the bread mother spent all day baking. Then, rather innocently, I mentioned how Jimmy Granite was picked up today by that man on the buggy.

Father nearly choked out the bread. "When did this happen? What time was it?"

Mother added, "did you go anywhere else after that; did you come straight home?"

"I just came home. Why? Did I do something wrong? Should we have gone with him? Do you know what happened to him?" I asked, without really wanting to know the details. It was one of those times I just wanted a yes or no answer. I should not have asked.

They looked at me for a minute, trying to decide how to explain the situation. Then, they tried… "Maybe we should call on them tomorrow." It was an odd ending to the meal, as well as the discussion. I felt like there was something not being said, and an explanation not being given. But I was okay with it at the time.

The next day was Saturday. No school was fine by me. Father and I went off to see Jimmy Granite's family, while mother went to the market, as she did just about every day.

When we got close to the Granite farm, father had me wait in the wagon while he went ahead. It was all quite strange, but he said he needed to know why the doctor's carriage was at the house, and he would just be a minute. So, I waited.

Maybe five minutes had passed and I began to get rather bored of this. I stepped down from the wagon and began to walk around to the back. Where I was standing, I must have been hidden from my father's view. When he returned, breathing heavily like he had just run back, he quickly started moving the wagon. I had to jump up on the wagon as he turned it about.

I yelled to wait, which he had. But when I climbed back on, he refused to explain anything from the Granite household. I had no idea what he had seen, and he would not likely be telling me any time soon.

When we returned home, mother was still out, which was not out of the ordinary. I kept asking Father, who looked a little like he had a secret he wanted to keep from me. He would not say. I assumed he would tell mother, so I decided to wait to hear what they wanted to say about it together. Any time we had a big thing happen in our lives, they often discussed things before I was told so I did not hear two different stories. When the war in Europe had started, they handled it that way. Same as when the United States decided to join the war. It put me at ease when they explained things this way, but very nervous in the build-up to the explanation.

Soon, mother came home and the two of them went upstairs to discuss things. I thought I would hear some loud discussion and maybe some disagreement. Not yelling, but not as quiet as it was. That actually worried me more than the last two times they did this.

When they came down the stairs, it seemed a very quiet eternity had passed. Father opened up with a simple explanation. "You cannot see Jimmy Granite any time soon. His family is sick."

"Okee doh-kee" was my simple response. Why say more? It was pretty obvious we would not be seeing him at school, so why would I go to his house and risk getting sick?

Mother chimed in, "Son, there is no reason for you to worry right now."

I wasn't worried. Not even sure why she said that.

"You can tell us what you are feeling," she would add.

"I am not feeling anything. I understand, he will be back to school in a few days, and we will see him then." I responded naively. It turns out I was wrong.

The next week was the week before my birthday. All my friends, minus Jimmy Granite were gathering around me every chance they had to ask me what I thought I was going to get for my birthday. I would not even guess, which was frustrating to them. Clarisse wanted me to say something expensive that we did not have the money to purchase, while Alan made a list of far more practical things. We would have a chance to consider all of these things each day on our way home.

Jeremy was reeling from the end of the relationship with Clarisse, so his input was little more than the most miserable of things. While others would suggest things like a new horse-cart, or horse (Clarisse), to some new tools or shoes (Alan), Jeremy was left to suggest things like a new sheet to bury my face in at night. So sad.

All week long, no one seemed to think about how long it had been since we had seen Jimmy Granite. It seemed a long time, just no one had actually put a number of days to it. We never thought to count the days at the time, but it would not have changed anything.

When I arrived home on Friday, exactly one week to the day when I had last seen Jimmy Granite, father was there, in the kitchen with mother. She was running around as she always did, but it seemed like she was working harder than usual doing so.

They told me the strangest thing. I had heard that Jimmy Granite's father had trouble and was actually getting worse. But… Jimmy Granite was not coming back to school anymore. He was... dead.

I just did not understand. Now I kept asking questions that my parents had expected from me earlier. I guess I was too excited about my birthday last week to get beyond that.

But now would not help anyone. Father had heard as many questions as he could and answered about half of them. Mother did not really stop moving about long enough to answer anything I had asked. She would stop every few minutes to clear her throat, as if to say something, but it never came.

The sickness, which seemed like a cough, with a fever, was over in Europe. The men who were serving the country were getting sick over there, some were saying it was a Spanish disease, and now it may have been coming back here with them. Maybe New York City, but not Pennsylvania. We lived in too small a village to worry about any of that, didn't we?

Jimmy Granite's father was actually at his son's funeral. He seemed a little sick, but his mother had said he was getting better, and was past the worst of it. They were so sad. We all were. That feeling just would not go away.

It was now three days until my birthday and everything had changed. My birthday list was just about pointless at this point. My parents would want me to have something of a gift, but maybe they would not even remember at this point.

Justin Jordan, Jeremy's older brother, had been scheduled to come back home from the war, but was stopped in New York for a period of quarantine. His letter said he would be in there for only a short period of time while they determined he did not have any disease, and then he would catch a train home. He was correct. We saw him coming from the train station just in time for dinner, as we came home from the church cemetery.

Father asked me what my friends thought about all of this. I could not really respond. We did not speak about this before, and it would be unlikely we would do so at school. Kids don't want to talk about anything but graduating at this point. And if any issues outside of my birthday would come up, Clarisse would squash it and come back to my birthday. I was starting to wonder if she liked me.

Mother could not eat that evening. She sat there with father and I, but just looked at us as we ate. Her complexion was pinker than usual, but no one wondered how she was feeling. At least not aloud.

"Son, please eat those peas from the garden. I picked them up from the market just this morning." Mother was going to market daily, so the routine did not seem like something like work for her. I actually thought she enjoyed it.

"Yes, mother" I replied dutifully. A few years ago, this would have been a battle if I was not in such a good mood. But, I had been saddened by the reality of Jimmy Granite, and the feeling from Jeremy, that the war may not be over any time soon. I would face a draft after my birthday. How could I not see that coming?

According to Jeremy, the enemy had advanced into parts we

had been and pushed us back. The offensive was always the last thing you would expect. You can take every precaution, prepare for the future, but the enemy comes at you when THEY want. And there is just about nothing you can do to be ready.

A draft had been around for some time. I was pretty sure it would be a long war, but this whole thing had never seemed like it would keep going beyond when I turned 18. And now…I was going to go off to war.

Clarisse had been talking more to me lately on my way home these days. It seemed inevitable that Jeremy would be offended at this, but he seemed to accept it. I think he was more interested in the war, since his big brother's return. He had been talking about it for days now. Nothing scary, just how happy he would be to serve his country if he was called.

He would not be. Apparently, he had flat feet. Something like that devastates boys like him. He would never be the same after he found out. But that would be for another time.

Clarisse was asking me about my parents just about every day. I think she was asking something about how they would respond to me dating a girl, or getting married. I was not disinterested, and it would be something to keep my mind off of other stuff.

Today was my birthday, and I was generally sad. I just could not shake the feeling of doom and gloom about my future. I would have to serve my country if called. Jeremy's dream would be mine, as I can't imagine I have flat feet. I had been a runner all my life. Loved to run, as fast as I could, wherever I wanted to go. There would be nothing wrong with my feet.

At home, mother and father were again sitting in the kitchen waiting for me. This was not good.

"Good afternoon" said mother, with a voice sounding more tired than I remembered it for this time of day. Her cheeks looking more rosy than the day before.

"Hulloo" I tried to say in my most cheerful voice.

Father said, "Son, you need to know that Jimmy Granite's

mother has just passed away. She died of that foreign flu. His father has not been seen for days now."

Such a gloomy greeting was getting to me. I was hoping they would have remembered my birthday. But news like this would put a damper on all of that.

Father then added, "please help your mother with dinner tonight, she could use the help." No problem with that. It would keep my mind off everything else. After dinner, they went to bed earlier than usual. Birthday forgotten, apparently. Oh well, it did not feel very joyous, anyway.

The next day, Saturday, was mother's usual market trip. But today would be different. I was going to the market for her, by myself. At 18, it should not be so unusual. After all, I am an adult and can go off to war, why would I not be able to purchase some vegetables, and chickens? We never needed any milk, Father took care of that with our cows. The rest of it would be easy enough to purchase at the market.

Mrs. Thun met me at the first stand and asked about my mother. She told me I was the spitting image of my father, and she did not forget to ask about my birthday. While that might make my parents sound like they were uncaring, Mrs. Thun was the mother of...my girlfriend, Clarisse. She was always very nice to me. Usually, when I had come to market as a young boy, with my mother, she had given me a small carrot, or some small apple she had, depending on the season. Clarisse was just like her mother, I guess.

Then, Mrs. Thun asked about my mother. I should have sensed something unusual in the question.

"She's a little tired today, so she asked me to come here and do some of the shopping." It was so matter-of-fact, that the answer stunned Mrs. Thun. She had been expecting even less than a reason for me to be at the market. As if I would be there just to see her, or as if I had nothing better to do. I did not, but that was beside the point.

"You had better make sure your mother is well. Here, take these apples home, they will be good for her." She shoved a few into my bag before I left. It all seemed typical enough, but it was now a gift for my mother, and not for me.

Upon arriving home, my father greeted me at the door. He was quite upset.

"Father, what is wrong?"

"Son, your mother is sick. You must stay outside the house for a little while until the doctor gets here." His concern was overwhelming.

I would not argue. I gave him the vegetables, and went for a walk. Not even sure where I was going at first, but once the sun came out, it warmed up and made me just want to run for a bit. As I began to run out of energy, I found myself at Clarisse's house. I wondered if she was about, so I knocked on the door.

"Hello, birthday boy!" She was home, and knew exactly how to cheer me up. Conversation with her was always cheery. This time, she made me completely forget all my troubles, until it was time to go home. It had gotten late as were talking, mostly outside on their tree swing. When I explained the situation with my mother, she told me I was worrying too much.

"She will be fine. Don't worry so much! Just because she is not feeling well does not mean it would be the flu." She was right. No reasonable person would jump to that conclusion.

We were both wrong. The doctor verified this on the front stoop of our house that very evening. After hearing the news, Father and I sat for a good ten minutes in silence. He was always having long discussions with me on the front porch, usually, as a follow-up to when I would have done something wrong as a child. This was definitely not the case this time. In fact, the tables seemed to have turned just a bit.

"Do me a favor and be quiet, please!" My father did not often yell, but now he was lashing out at me. He wanted to make my mother better, and could not find a way to do it now.

How was that fair? I had just about opened my mouth when he just yelled that at me. It wasn't like I was the one who started the whole thing. I had not made my mother sick. But, one could become easily confused at these times. After all, the whole world seemed to be coming apart.

CHAPTER TWO

Mother was going to be away for a few days, so father had Aunt Shirley come stay with me while he set up a little bed at the town infirmary. We had no hospital in our village, and the nearest town had an infirmary where folks could stay overnight for medical care if they needed it. Mostly, this kind of thing was for any person who was thought to be very sick and should not stay at home. While I was no longer a child, technically, I was still living at home and attend school for the time being. So, Mother had to go there, at least for a few days.

Aunt Shirley lived about a day's ride away and could not be here until the weekend. For the time being, it was just me, and I was going to take care of father. The task was pretty big, considering I did not really know much about preparing dinner. I could shop at the market, and tend to the cows okay, but the dinners were always my mother's area of expertise. I had seen a few things in the past, like lighting the fire burning stove, drawing some water from the pump into a pot and getting that all set up to boil. I did not know what to boil, or why for that matter. But I could at least get the water boiling. I was pretty proud of that, actually.

Everyone I spoke to was pretty sure mother would be okay, and that she just needed rest. Father was most cheerful, for at least the first two days, telling me she will be just fine. He may have been more worried about getting food ready for us. But that was what neighbors were for!

"Good afternoon Mrs. Sincavage! How can I help you?" I addressed the next-door-neighbor as politely as I could, despite the ravenous hunger I felt all afternoon, and the fact that she was clearly carrying a large dinner dish meant for Father and me.

"Oh, dear boy, where is your father?" She asked as we moved inside, all the while she clung to that dish, hoping to surprise my father with it. We went over to the kitchen table and she set the pot down. It was filled with something she called chicken pot pie. I did not understand the "pie" part of that name. It was NOT a pie, just chicken inside a pot with some dough and chicken gravy all throughout. It was delicious, just NOT a pie.

"He should be home soon," I replied, "just coming back from seeing mother. Mrs. Sincavage looked absolutely saddened when I told her he would not be here to see how kind she had been to bring this feast for us. I knew he would be very hungry, as we would always eat dinner around this hour.

"Well, dear boy, please keep the lid on, and keep it warm. Do you know how to do that?" Mrs. Sincavage was always trying to take care of everyone around the neighborhood. This was no exception. A couple years back, after her son, Tommy had run away to join the circus, she was pretty much left alone in the house. The neighbors all got together and decided to take care of her, but she put a stop to that right away by bringing dinners to everyone else's house within the week. Seems that since Old Man Sincavage died of some disease no one talked about, she had been obsessed with taking care of the boy, Tommy. Now that he was gone, she tried to care for everyone else. It was kind of sweet, if not a bit unnecessary. But, tonight, I was quite happy about it!

"I can take care of that. Thank you very much!" Which I either said with too little sincerity, or she did not believe that I really knew how to take care of putting a pot in the oven? Either way, she simply moved about the kitchen and just put things in places where I did not even knew they went. All the while, keeping an eye on the chicken dish that she had placed in the oven for me. Oh, well, who was I to argue? Food was coming and I was hungry.

What seemed like an eternity had passed, and Mrs. Sincavage had finally left the house in an order that she called "shipshape".

I thought I knew what she meant, maybe something like "not the way your mother would have left it", but at least it did not look the way I had it for the past two days.

Father arrived soon after and looked very tired. "Hello, Father" I greeting him with the most cheerful voice I could muster. It was getting dark, and for late March, that was starting to look later and later.

"Hello, son." He sounded exhausted. "What is that terrific smell?" He was obviously referring to Mrs. Sincavage's chicken pot pie. It did smell delicious.

We soon ate, cleared the table and I got the chore of cleaning up the bowls. Father would sleep sooner and longer than usual, but considering how tired he had looked, I was not surprised.

The next morning a knock on the door, just about the time the first milking was finished. Our cows got milked two times per day, at least regularly. Every so often, father would have one or two who needed an additional time, but that was never something I could take care of while at school.

"Oh how are you, you dear boy?" It was Aunt Shirley and she had bags of food along with her. Thank goodness, I was hungry again.

"I am just fine. How are you? How was your ride?" Aunt Shirley had some money, and where she lived, most people had developed a fascination with the Model T. She had driven hers to our house, which accounts for how fast she had made it here this morning.

"Lovely, quite lovely, thank you! I suppose your father is visiting your mother across town? How would you like one of my famous egg breakfasts?" As I was very hungry, I would not dream of arguing that it was not so famous.

We spent most of the day eating and sharing stories from the past few months. I told her about Jimmy Granite and Clarisse, while she regaled me with stories of how wonderful life was like in a city. Reading sounded wonderful to hear her tell about it.

Pretzels and wonderful hillside resorts, amusement rides, and very successful factories - it was all too wonderful to hear her tell it. The sounds of Reading were probably akin to the grinding sound of her car being cranked to start. Which I was going to learn… This morning.

Once I had figured out how to "put my back into it", we were on our way. Our village was so small, that we were at Clarisse's house in five minutes. I usually just walked it, but it took me about twenty minutes to get there. It was easier for me to see her mother at the open market, which was in the center of town, behind the church grounds.

The scenery passed by excitingly fast, as if we were on a galloping horse, but without the wind in my face. There was a window for that. It was a bit loud, but I did not mind. After all, I did not have to knock on the door this way; Clarisse heard me before we came to a complete stop.

I introduced Aunt Shirley, saying "My mother's sister", which technically was not correct, but nobody in town knew any better. She was actually her cousin, but when Shirley's parents had passed, she went to live with mother's family.

Aunt Shirley was absolutely wonderful. She was so nice to Clarisse, offering to take us both for a ride, as long as we agreed to run the crank to get the car started up. Everywhere we would go, it seemed Clarisse was completely excited about. "Oh, the market! Let's see mother!" "Oh, the school! Isn't it a pretty building!" Which was maybe a little too excited at the time, but I was enjoying this far too much to care.

After a long day, we returned Clarisse to her house and returned back to the house. Father would be home soon, so I took care of the afternoon milking, and Aunt Shirley prepared the dinner. It was the nicest afternoon I had in a while. Then, father arrived, and that all began to change.

"Father, you look very tired again. Maybe you should have a rest before dinner?"

"No, son, I am far too hungry to skip dinner. Let's eat first, then to bed. Are the cows well? Any excitement here while I am away?" His voice began to trail off, and he seemed to choke a bit. Not that I had noticed much at the time, but he was not looking well at all.

"Father, the cows are fine. Today, Aunt Shirley took us around town in her automobile. We collected Clarisse and ventured around the village. It was a nice time." Perhaps I had been too happy about it.

"Very well son. Very well." He did not ask anything else. He was finished talking for the evening. It was unlike him. We usually had more discussion than that, but he was not going to say anything more. At the time, I honestly did not notice a problem with it.

The next day, father was gone before I awoke. Should we go about our daily routines and not see each other until the evening, the day would seem to be off to a fairly normal start. There would be a bucket at the back of the kitchen door telling me to take care of the cows, nothing new.

When I came back inside, Aunt Shirley greeted me with a very concerned expression. "We need to talk," sounding very much like mother and father when something that was coming that was a pretty big deal.

"Yes, Aunt Shirley" I was now cautious and a bit concerned. It was not like her to be anything less than fun, often exciting. This was a new side of her, and I did not like it.

"Your father is not coming back this evening, I'm afraid" she said plainly.

"That is no problem, I can take care of the cows, myself!" I wanted to show her how grown up I was, and that I can prove to her how easy this could be. We just had to keep doing what we had been doing and nothing needed to change.

"That would be terrific, if he was only gone for a short time. But we have no idea when he may return, I am afraid." That did not sound good.

"What, exactly do you mean?"

"Dear boy, he is sick and has gone to the infirmary. He will be with your mother there. She is not doing very well, either."

I suddenly felt like a giant stone had fallen on my head. Neither of my parents was coming home for I-don't-know-how-long, and...and I just don't know what is happening now.

"We will stay here through the end of the school year, and see what happens next" she breathed out, exhausted, as if she was the sick one.

"Yes, Aunt Shirley" which was just about all I could muster. I could say nothing else. I was hardly aware of anything for the rest of the day, except taking care of the cows.

I am not even sure how I got to school on Monday, but I was there. The day seemed like it had passed before I was aware of scenery, school work, or teachers. It was only my friends on the walk home who helped me realize what had become of my life.

"Honestly, you are quite lucky you have an Aunt Shirley" said Clarisse. She was right. Aunt Shirley would be the one person I wanted to be around. She would be fun and could brighten up my day no matter what. I was sure we would spend our days driving around in that Model T of hers, and we would occasionally gather up some of my friends and see everyone in the village. I thought that might last all spring and summer. Boy, was I wrong…

CHAPTER THREE

The ride over the mountain was long, but considering all the changes you might see between village life and the big town of Reading, not as long of a ride as you might expect. It was as if we had gone to another world to get here. I miss seeing the farms, the natural state of the roads, being dirt-covered with all of the ruts that I know how to avoid better than most. The bouncing around we often felt on those wagon rides was now much smoother, but I have been told that is because we hit bumps faster. A few streets were lined with cobblestones, which required a slower drive. But travelling around in Reading was like an altogether different experience than back in the village.

It had been several weeks since I arrived in Reading. The city was very active, and as far as I could tell it looked like a pretty amazing place. The people were very nice here, and the town had some big businesses around that had to be relatively successful. Many people seemed to have cars, mostly Model T's, and that made the whole place look like another world to me. Compared to my home village, where everyone was still going around in horse-drawn wagons, this place looked like a futuristic land.

People were walking the streets, while horse-drawn wagons were still on the roads. Yet, many were driving around in automobiles, all at the same time. The main street in the middle of town, named after the founder of Pennsylvania, William Penn, was as busy as I could have imagined any place to be. I was shocked at how many people were moving about up and down the street. There were stores and markets and places that appealed to just about every taste imaginable.

I am convinced that we had driven the car through the entire city by that point. I saw many large buildings, each more impressive than the last. The city had a building that held the entire county courthouse, which I have heard about in stories before. Several farm owners from our village had to go there a few years back. I think they came to Reading to argue about some taxes or something. I did not follow the details too closely, but now I see where they went. Their descriptions of that place did not fully paint a picture of how big the whole thing looked from the street.

The Courthouse building was three stories tall, which you just did not see in the village. It had about fifteen windows on each floor facing Penn's Street. Compared to just two or three on some or our village's biggest buildings, this place just looked massive to me. It was mostly brick, which was also not something you saw very often outside of Reading. Our buildings were mostly wood or stone, except for a few smaller outbuildings, like kitchens, so this brick structure's construction was truly a rare sight for a building that was so large.

There was a square in the middle of town, where it seemed a similar marketplace to the farmer's market in the village, only a much bigger and broader venue for all the people who live in the city. Actually, the city had stores that fronted the main street, which was just like our town market. I recognized the area from Aunt Shirley's description of the place. They seemed to have everything for sale, from baskets to glass-filled jars of food, to ground spices, to birds in cages, to flowers, to prepared foods like fried chicken dinners. The people in the city market were all so very friendly, each offering to give samples of the things they were selling. I could have had a taste of German mashed potatoes, to Bavarian pretzels, to something called an Italian meatball, to a Polish pierogi. It was all so amazing to see so much available in such a large market. Our village offered a market of locally grown foods, while this city market looked like things from all around the world. It was truly a marvel.

One storefront appeared to be packed with people. I had to really stare, which I know was rude, but I just could not help myself. The window looked like it would practically burst from all the folks standing around. They were all shouting and laughing. At first, I could not even tell if they were happy or angry. The noise was quite something. At a glance, you may have even missed the glasses that all the patrons were holding, which was clearly the reason for them to be all gathered around inside.

This establishment was one of many breweries in Reading, and it was obviously a well-attended one that did not hurt for business. I wanted to ask what "happy hour" was, but looking at the sign, it looked pretty clear to me it had to do with the beer that flowed from inside this barroom. The brand, named after the city itself, Reading, was the same brand I often saw Jimmy Granite's father's hand wrapped around. I began to think about how the man was coping with the loss of Jimmy, but that was a little too sad for me to ponder while watching all those happy people inside.

Aunt Shirley told me that I had to finish school, which I did. Well, at least I tried. The school back home would have been at the point where we finished all of our lessons by now, and I would have graduated. I was certain to have good grades, and I would have been one of the first to study for any tests we would have taken. I would have done well on those tests, too. Only, I did not take any tests now. We had begun some lessons from a book Aunt Shirley had borrowed from a place called a library. We looked at the book a few times, but it did not tell us anything I needed to know which I had not already learned. The effort we made seemed to be enough, and she said we could be done.

While many of my fellow classmates were finishing lessons in both the boys' school and the girls' sister-school, I knew I might be missing a few activities, but no really important lessons. I would miss seeing some of them, for sure. I would also not miss seeing a few of them, which made me feel a little better about not being there.

I honestly missed the daily cow-milking. You tend to become somewhat attached to the cows after you are so close to them every day. One of the cows had given birth some time ago and then disappeared. Father said she went looking for her "husband", but I never really believed that to be true. I think she died and he did not want to talk about it with me, as I was so young at the time. He thought I would cry or something. I don't think I would have, but now I appreciate what he had tried to do for me.

The cow had a baby, which we named Joey. He thought he was our pet, I suppose. He followed us everywhere, which would be just like a pet would have done. He jumped around us whenever we were in the fenced in cow pen, and when we were out in the pasture, he managed to find us. The pasture was pretty large, to allow for the cows to range freely along the creek, under some trees, and open grasses. Joey had to be intent on finding us to have run around that whole area and found us every day. He would respond to our voices and began to get somewhat aggressive around the other cows when we touched them. Father became uncomfortable around him, while I started to really become attached to him. Perhaps that was problematic, but with no dogs around our house, it was as close to a real pet as I was going to get. Mother said Joey thought we were his family. Since he was a bull calf, which of course is the name for a future bull, we had to send him away from our female animals. It was a sad day. Now, I really missed Joey.

The herd was being tended by the neighbors now. I would not see them soon, but we were all sure they would be fine. I missed the activity of tending them, little Joey, and not much else from our village. I began to think of it as another time in my life that was in the past. It was as if I would not go back there again.

Today was Sunday, and Aunt Shirley had been excited about taking me to her church. The building was in the center of

Reading. It was a very tall building, with a white steeple about a hundred feet tall. It looked like the tallest building I had ever seen. It was so tall that you could see the white steeple from the mountain. It was the first thing I had seen when we first came into the city and I was rather impressed by the splendor of it from afar. I was no less impressed when I walked into the building on Sunday.

The service was much like the few my father and mother had taken me to when I was a kid. Only in this building, it seemed even more grand. We have not really been to church very often in the past. Aunt Shirley said that was not what they had learned to do when she was a child. She seemed disappointed we had not gone to church more often and said while I lived with her that was going to change. I did not mind hearing that. She cared for me, and I liked that now that my parents were not around.

The service was simple enough. I could not tell you what the pastor said about anything. Not that I did not listen, I just do not recall much of it. I don't think I could relate to anything. But that may have been because I was still so taken aback by the splendor of the actual building. As it turned out, it was kind of a strange place. It was a very old, historic building, with some colonial American history to it. I did not bother to find out more of the details, I was just not that interested at the time. There were many folks inside the church who did not seem to be particularly friendly to me, and that was all I noticed while we were there, after I got past the grandeur of the setting. Aunt Shirley only said hello to a couple people, so not too many people would be friendly to me, either. I was surprised Aunt Shirley seemed to keep to herself in the church. She opened a prayer book and never really looked back up until the sermon.

There were a few comments by the minister about a person who just died of the flu, although he was not a member of this church. I was a little surprised to hear it. The village had been like the other side of the world to these people, but this illness had made its way here, too. The minister seemed to think fresh air would help people, along with a healthy dose of faith in God. At that moment, I was not inclined to agree. You could not argue my parents had anything less than a healthy dose of fresh air on our small farm.

When the church service was all over, we talked to a few more people and we left. The folks at church were nice enough to me, if not a bit short with their greetings, following the pastor's orders to keep conversations short so we could all get outside for the best of our health. Some had accents that I did not recognize, coming from other parts of the world. That was what I was expecting to hear, actually. I fully expected most of Reading to sound different. Most of the county had come from Germany at one point, calling themselves Pennsylvania Dutch or German. But Reading had people from all over the place. Some were from England, some from Italy and a few were even from eastern Europe. It was all very interesting to hear them speak.

They were very polite with their brief comments. The minister had also mentioned something about keeping a distance in this time, and people in the church were following this, much more so than the folks in town going about their daily tasks. As it turned out, it was good advice. Keeping our distance was supposed to keep us away from others who may be sick. The flu was all over the place, including Reading.

It felt good to be at church. It was almost like being apart from all the problems I had encountered in the world. Like I was just insulated from the things that were going on in my life. It was not as if there were no difficulties in my life, just that I felt like they could not touch me while I was here. I liked it so much, I told Aunt Shirley we needed to come back to church next week. And maybe every Sunday after that, too.

As we got back to the house, I realized how lucky I had been to not get sick. Father and mother would be returning to the house when they were healthier, but I would not be allowed to return until they sent for me. I could still get sick from them. Everyone thought a good, hot summer could be harmful, and might not stop the spread of disease in our small village. Everyone was correct. But the city of Reading would not be much safer as it turned out.

People who took care of getting milk to your home, called "milkmen" were supposedly spreading the disease, so Aunt Shirley asked to not get milk for a few days, until people told her it was safe again. I was happy to have the milk again. It was one of the few things I had to remind me of home.

When we came home from church we often sat outside on the front porch. Aunt Shirley's home sat on the hillside, looking down into the town. We enjoyed the view that first day, watching people in their hustle and bustle around town, and neighbors tidying up around the house at the end of their weekends. It was rather picturesque and relaxing.

At the time, I little realized how much that would change for me. It would not be for some time that any of us might be that relaxed again.

CHAPTER FOUR

Clarisse clearly missed seeing me on those walks home from school. She missed spending time with me, and as we had ended things rather abruptly, she was confused as to what had happened. Her letter even asked me what she had done wrong and why I was angry with her to have left that way.

I could not understand that last part. It was a mess before I left. Aunt Shirley grabbed me and as much stuff as we could carry, and we took off for Reading in an attempt to get away from the house as quickly as possible. Turns out, it may have been a good idea. We got out of the village before the flu began to infect more people there. Not to say I would have been next, but it was a good thing I would not be there to find out.

However, my fast exit was a bad sign for Clarisse. She had thought I left quickly and quietly to avoid seeing her. I really did not think about that when I left and now, I felt kind of badly about it. I did not know how to handle that situation, other than to write a letter to her and explain that I could not return any time soon.

As I considered how to respond to her, I gathered up my emotions and began to write to her. I was surprised at what came from my hand. There was some element of longing and loneliness that seeped into that letter that I had not considered until putting pen to paper. If that was all true, and I had no reason to believe I was lying to her, I cared for her rather deeply. I did not even realize that was the case. I just did not know she had affected me that way.

I had a long walk to the mailbox and thought more about missing her with every step. It physically hurt me when I placed the envelope into the box. I was reeling from the ache I had felt. It made no sense. The last time I had seen her was not too long ago, yet it seemed like forever. Her face was the only thing I could see when I closed my eyes. Was that weird? After all, I had not seen my mother or father in just about the same time, but I did not miss them nearly as much. I was seriously questioning my sanity at this point.

The dinner discussion with Aunt Shirley was centered on what I would be doing now that school was over. I kept thinking about Clarisse, and I just did not know why. When Aunt Shirley asked me about my plans, I just shrugged. I had not thought much about it. She was not too happy to hear that, of course. There was not much I wanted to do. I had always just assumed I would be milking cows, like my father, and his father before him. I wanted nothing more than that before all this stuff happened, and I never had expected that to change.

She was blunt and honest with me, which was one of the qualities I loved about her. We had grown closer and she allowed me to see more of her than just the "fun" side that I had always thought was her true nature. She was somehow deeper than that, and was constantly showing it these days. "Your parents may not be returning any time soon. Would that change your plans?" That one hurt; kind of poked at me right in the gut, like so many times Clarisse elbowed me when I teased her. I suppose it was more like flirting, but I never really thought of that when I was doing it.

"Well, yes, of course it would. I would not have the cows to attend if there was no farm." But I thought of that as more like fantasy than reality. It was just a matter of time until mother and father returned, so that would be when we would all be reunited and life would continue on the farm. It was not really much of a farm, just a pasture, a stream, our modest home, which always seemed large enough to me before I came to Reading.

Then something strange happened. No idea why, but I felt a tear roll down my cheek. I knew I had to feel badly about the whole situation, but I was always told not to feel sorry for myself. I was not particularly sad, was I? I had not thought much about the future of our farm, or when my mother and father would return, but it seems there was a glimmer of hopelessness in my soul that just peeked out for a moment. It took little effort to suppress it, and I quickly and quietly did just that. Aunt Shirley would not notice. Or else she did not want to notice.

"So, what would you consider doing while you are here in Reading? Shall we look for a job somewhere? You seem to like automobiles quite a bit; would you consider working on them, as, say a mechanic?"

"Umm, yes ma'am." The response just came out of me without much thought. Did I really want to work on automobiles? I don't think that was something I had ever intended to do, but I did like these Model Ts. She took my response in stride and we moved the conversation along. Neither of us dwelt on that answer more than necessary. We did not think of that as the direction my life would take, just an option that would be considered if it came to it.

The conversation was fairly brief after that. Aunt Shirley did not want to push that idea, as I did not think she wanted to have a child of her own. She did not have a husband...any more...so, she would not want to take care of a child. Come to think of it, I must have seemed like a bit of a burden. All this time, I was sleeping in the guest room, and I was treated like her son would have been treated, I suppose. Never had I thought of how this might be affecting her. She had been acting differently lately. While at first, it seemed like she was being blunt, honest and open with me, I began to think perhaps it was something more. Maybe she was getting irritated that I was here all the time and she had to take care of me? This made me wonder the reasons for her asking me to look into a job as an automobile mechanic.

If she was to treat me more like her own son, things may start to change around here. I did not want that. I was still holding out hope that the more fun parts of Aunty Shirley would come back as we got more comfortable with our new situation.

It could not be that she wanted me to go out on my own and become an adult. That was my parent's job. She was not my mother, nor did she act like she wanted to be that. We were always more like friends than relatives. She would come up with fun ideas and we would do them. It was always something wild and exciting with her. We would always find something new to do and nobody had ever thought about doing it that way before. When we picked strawberries, she became the catcher and I, the pitcher in a game of baseball.

As we got to church the other day, she came up with a story about what every group of people was saying as they got out of their vehicles and walked into the church, while we sat in our Model T. One time, as the milkman came to deliver the milk, Aunt Shirley acted like the milk was poison and he was trying to kill us. It was all just good fun.

I began to wonder what had happened to her that she was acting this way: so much less fun all of a sudden. I could not imagine I had done anything to change her opinion of me. I had not been particularly lazy, completing all sorts of chores around the house. Although some were more complicated than others, I did them all with no -- make that little -- complaint.

I hated dusting furniture, as mother made me do on occasion at our house. But I did it, nonetheless. It would not be rational to assume she would want me around if all I did was complain and never did any work around here, so I kept up what I thought to be my fair share of the work.

She never said I should do it all over again, or that it was not adequate. Therefore, I assumed it had to have been good enough. Dusting aside, I was a help in the kitchen, I swept up the floors when asked, and even cleaned out the fireplace, which was a very dirty job. No, completing chores around here was not a problem for me, and it would not be the reason Aunt Shirley wanted me to get a job. I did not give that much more thought for the evening.

Instead, I got out a paper and started writing again. This letter to Clarisse would be different. I was not going to be all sweet and nice, but honest and forthcoming with my situation here in Reading. How things had gone so far was not as anyone had intended, but it was our new reality. I wanted her to know what she meant to me in planning for the future.

"I want you to know you are in my thoughts as I consider creating a life here in Reading. I did not want to have a new beginning here, I see little choice until my parents return. I cannot change my situation, but I also do not want to do this without you around. We are not going to be able to change any of this any time soon."

No changes expected soon. Plenty of time ahead of us in this same situation, may as well get used to it. How sad the whole thing started to seem. I was not one to feel bad for myself and get all depressed with my situation in life. Up to this point, I had little reason to feel that way about anything. My life was nice and I was a pretty happy person. So, now that everything had gone differently than I expected, it would test me and my ability to stay that happy-go-lucky kid that my Aunt Shirley thought she was taking with her back to Reading.

I decided to make the letter shorter than first anticipated. I was not sure what more I wanted to say, and rather than go on about my feelings for her again, I just ended it. I could write again tomorrow if I wanted. This would be fine. She would understand.

The next day I walked to the mailbox in a much more assured stride. I felt better, the sun was shining on a wonderful summer's day, the world was full of possibility, and the day was looking bright. The whole setting was cheerful, which I needed. I would not get down by thinking of my future. There was no reason to do so. And when I opened up the mailbox, everything changed.

CHAPTER FIVE

The letter we had been waiting for from father and mother had finally arrived. They had been sent home, and had been well enough to write! I was excited, if not a bit sad to have to leave my Aunt Shirley alone again.

Aunt Shirley's husband, Peter had been a very healthy and active young man years ago. He was involved in a lot of activities in the community, in the church. I think he was the kind of guy you hear about that no one says a bad thing about. I suppose he could have run for mayor of Reading, had things turned out differently. Which maybe makes this whole story much more depressing.

Peter was one of the first Americans who volunteered to go to France and fly planes to help the French people in their struggle against the Kaiser. At first, we did not understand how anyone from a place called Pennsylvania Dutch Country would ever be so excited about fighting the Germans. After all, "Dutch" meant German, and he was born and raised right here in Reading, Pennsylvania. But there was much more involved in this story.

Peter, like my father, was also a huge history buff and learned a lot about his family's history. His grandmother was from an area of France called Alsace-Lorraine, which had been taken from France by the Germans in the Franco-Prussian War. He had never known her, nor had he even been out of the country before. But he felt some kind of kinship to her that made him angry at this land of his ancestors being lost to the Germans. So, he was actually French, not completely German as many people here were. And it was because of that relationship that Peter decided to travel to France and support the French cause in protecting them from getting completely taken over by the invading Germans.

The United States was still a few years away from entering this war. One thing I recall was President Wilson saying that he loved peace and would keep us out of war. Peter was enraged by that. He acted as if France would be gone by the time the U.S. entered the war. So, he packed up his things, learned a few French words and got on the first boat to France.

His letters came every day for the first couple weeks, at least according to my aunt. She was so proud of him and missed him dearly. They had only been married a short time when this all came to be. When his letters slowed, they began to sound different. I cannot truly explain the reason for the change, but I have come up with a guess as to why. The letters began to involve less information and more emotions. Peter was rather emotional, and these letters may have been more sad than before. Almost as if he saw things happening that he could not change over there, and he had begun to accept the changes being beyond his control, and that just made him sad. He stopped writing one day, and that was the last we had ever heard from him.

For a time, my aunt put her mind into factory work, of which there was lots in town at the time. She did not want to think anything happened to him. In fact, we never really knew if anything actually did happen. He just stopped writing, and we never heard anything more. She did not act like she expected him to come home, but had somehow moved on with her life. It was like we never spoke of him again. But I am sure he had not been forgotten forever.

After our time together, which had been about four months now, we have grown pretty close. We went to our July 4th parade together and she and I dressed in red, white, and blue, waved American flags and saluted the Spanish American War veterans as they marched down Penn's Avenue. It was a glorious day, and awfully hot, too!

We spent our Sundays at church, praying for my parents, and I began to pray for Peter, too. All the while the minister's asking us to keep our distance from other folks, seems to have done some good. The city seems to have gotten healthy again. In fact, some people were saying this Spanish Flu has now passed us by. We would be healthier now, and the war had not killed as many Americans as we were afraid it might. We seemed to have turned a corner and brighter days were ahead!

Now I would be packing up, heading back to the village, and entering back into my former life. The last few months were great, but reality was coming back into my life. I could imagine the changes and I would not fight them. I would miss my aunt, but she could always visit me. She would probably go back to being my "fun" aunt now that it would be less time around each other. Now that she was not acting the role of my parent, she would certainly go back to being that fun-loving aunt I always enjoyed when I was a kid. At least I could imagine the brighter side of this relationship, hopefully she could, too.

Aunt Shirley sat in the rocking chair she was left by my grandparents, and re-read the letter several times. She acted calm and smiled peacefully. I guess she may have actually been relieved. I knew we had grown closer, there was no denying that. We had really grown close in the past few months. But had I been so self-absorbed that all I could envision at this time was my aunt missing me? Was there something I had missed in this relationship that was beyond just the aunt-nephew relationship?

She was pleased that I was leaving...I never considered that she may not have wanted me around. But her appearance, the placid look on her face at the thought of me going back home was something that caught me off-guard. I was devastated. Time stood still...

I did not want to upset her, but I did not know what to do at this point. So, I left the front porch, went back into the house and just sat there. Total quiet, total self-reflection, totally into my own head. I had to come up with something to say to Aunt Shirley, that made her not dislike having me around.

Yet, again, she saved me. She came into the parlor and sat next to me on the settee. Put her hand on my shoulder and smiled. She had never, not once thought of her own feelings. I read it all wrong. She was so thrilled for me to get back to my father and mother, that she immediately thought how that would benefit me and my parents. It was the least selfish thing one could possibly have moving through one's mind.

Aunt Shirley had only thought of me and my parents. That explained the peaceful look of relief on her face. She was happy for us, and was actually feeling a bit sad for herself, at being left alone again. Now, I felt foolish. I can't believe my only thought was about myself.

I had to apologize to her about what went through my head. It was so wrong and it would be something I regretted deeply. And, of course she laughed, "Oh, silly, it's fine! Of course, I understand your feelings. I am so sorry you thought that. But I will miss you more than you will miss me. I am just so happy you will get your parents back."

Turns out it would be a few more weeks while my parents recovered until I could get home to them. But for the time being, we would continue my brief education on the engine of a Model T automobile. And we would keep going to church together and travel about the town of Reading.

July went fast. These days were hot, sweltering days, with only a few cool nights to take off the edge of that humidity we were feeling. We had to move our beds to the first floor to make it less sweltering throughout the week. All the while, we considered some activities for evenings and weekends to make the time pass quicker. Reading had a baseball team we went to see.

Baseball was always a fun activity for people in town, but not the kind of thing we played back in the village in any kind of organized way. I tried to play baseball a few times when a few of the village kids got together, but it was not very realistic. Some of the older kids changed the rules during the game, and it never even looked like baseball at the end of the day. Fun, yes, baseball, not so much.

The Reading Cardinals baseball team had home games almost every Sunday in the month of July. We went to the game after church one Sunday. We had a great view, about three rows behind the first baseman. We arrived early, to hear a young lady sing the Star-Spangled Banner, see the mayor throw out the first pitch, and watch the Reading Cardinals dominate the first inning of play. They scored a full six runs before the inning even ended. It was exciting play to watch, despite the turn of events going against Reading at the tail end of the inning, with a double-play to end the first.

One of the most amazing things was having salesmen offering peanuts and hot dogs as they passed by us in the stands. How exciting the experience was to be able to eat a hot dog without even getting up from our seats! No need to even get up, except for when a foul ball was popped up in our direction. We did not catch it.

A very young fan to my right had a baseball hat on, although I did not recognize the team logo. He was holding a very small baseball pennant in his right hand, and a kid-sized catcher's glove in the other. His father was feeding him a hot dog while they cheered for every single pitch. It was all very amusing to me.

At the end of the fifth inning, it was getting really hot. It felt like I was melting to the seat. Aunt Shirley said we could go. She was getting pretty warm, too. Once we got up from the seats, we began to cool off. The Reading ballpark was very close to Aunt Shirley's home on Centre Avenue. It did not take long to get home. And it was pretty hot at home, too. No real relief there, either. At least we were out of the sun.

CHAPTER SIX

The letter said it is time to come home. We were expecting that soon, and here it was. We spent the entire day putting our stuff into piles. It was funny that in this short time, some of my things were so intertwined with Aunty Shirley's that we had to spend a few hours trying to figure out what was mine and what was hers.

We packed up the automobile and got in. It would not start right away and I got to show her what I had learned. It was nothing that would take long, so we got on our way and that was that. Reading would be behind me now. Literally and figuratively.

The trip took very little time compared to how long it seemed to take going to Reading in the first place. The first glimpse of the village was kind of sad. It brought back some fond memories, of course, but as I saw it from the Model T, it made me think of sad things, like missing my friends, our last days of school that we could have been together, and, of course, the death of my friend Jimmy Granite. The village would never seem the same to me.

It was such a small place now that I had lived in Reading. Taking our time to get across the main street and down to my house, Aunt Shirley said she would really miss me. Now I knew that was true.

My parents were very happy to see me. They looked well-rested and very comfortable moving about at our home. Nothing made me worry about their health any more. I was very happy about that. I would not be concerned about them anymore. They would be fine.

Aunt Shirley was relieved to see them, as well. She stayed the night and would return back to Reading tomorrow.

The next day, mother and Aunt Shirley made father and I a very big breakfast, including eggs and toast, with bacon that mother cooked in her trusty iron skillet. I could hardly pick that thing up when she was teaching me how to clean it years ago. Now, I don't remember a thing about how to clean it, let alone how to cook bacon in it.

Mother was a master at cooking it just right. She made it just a bit browned on the edges, without burning it all black. She had found a side of bacon she liked, which had been cured, salted and smoked by the Levengud family on the other side of the market. They brought their pork products to market every Thursday to sell. Mother was always there first, sometimes waiting for the Levenguds to place the open sign on the counter to begin the day.

Mother would always talk about how the weather was the day before and what we might expect the weather to be like today. Then they would discuss the kids, me as well as the Levengud twins who were about three years older. Dan was the boy twin. He was drafted to serve in the Army, but somehow went to the Navy, instead. Apparently, that was considered a smarter option for him.

I did not know how that would work for me, but as we were still waiting to hear from the draft board, I could not worry about it now.

Mother never once spoke a word about her pork orders after she gave a look around. Something like her bacon order was just known to the Levenguds. They just had it ready for her as if it was a standing appointment. No words seemed necessary. It was just a matter-of-fact that she wanted it the way she wanted it, and that was not going to change. And, furthermore, the Levenguds knew exactly what she wanted, as if the words were not needed.

The conversation that did take place, despite never being about her actual order, was pretty predictable. I always found if funny how that bacon order was like the coming of the time of day on the face of a clock. It was always the same, and everyone just knew it.

As mother cooked her bacon, the wonderful smells of the fatty salty, crispy meat wafted throughout the house. It was enough to make everyone hungry, of course. Which I suspect was always the best way to make sure we ate it all and left no food on the table. Nothing quite tasted as good as mother's breakfasts. I did not realize how much I missed them until that moment I entered the kitchen.

Mother was wearing her Saturday-chores clothing. It was a bit like an everyday outfit, but not quite designed for simply working around the house. She was ready to out to the market again and pick up the vegetables and fruits. Apparently, there were some fresh fruits for mid-July that needed some picking and the farmers market would have them within minutes of coming off the vines.

Aunt Shirley was dressed to drive. She wore a beautiful scarf with pinks and blues, which really brought out the blue in her eyes. She was quite an attractive woman, actually. It was a shame her husband was now gone, but she would not have a problem finding a new one if she wanted. Mother often said that about her. After spending so much time with her lately, I had to agree. I would really miss her.

Father and I got to milking the cows. I noticed that maybe two of them were not there. Father said he left one with the neighbors, sort of as a payment as taking care of them. I agreed that was a good move on his part, but that did not explain where the other cow was. I assumed she had somehow not made it through the hot month and just passed away. Cows have as tough a time as humans with this weather, so that would not be much of a stretch to see this as a tough time for them. I did not ask any more questions. It did make me further question mortality.

Funny, but only a short time ago I felt like nothing in the world could hurt me. Now that had all changed. I could not look upon life quite the same way again. It was brief and precious. Nothing had prepared me for what we went through these past few months and I had no idea that it may actually get worse in the coming months.

Clarisse was very happy to see me. That was expected. I was happy to see her, but it was not the same. I had been through a few events in the past couple of months that she had not, and I could not share that with her. We had simply lived different lives for a time, and I did not feel as close to her as I had before. I was sure that would change, and we could see each other more often now. It felt like our time together would increase over the next few months and we might actually grow closer.

She was taking care of her hair in a different way now. I could not say what she had done differently, but I really liked it. A new style, a different cut, a new curl, a lighter color...whatever it was, it made her look older and more mature. It stirred feelings in me that I did not know I had. I could not stop staring at her. She was beautiful.

We walked down to the creek at the bottom of our property and just talked. It was a nice day. We held hands as we walked in the shade of the trees along the creek. I did not really care if anyone saw us together as a couple before, but now I was happy to have everyone see us together. It was as if I was bragging that she was my girlfriend now. I almost wanted to shout aloud, "Yes, she is mine!"

Clarisse wanted to discuss where we could live when we were married. It was the first time she used the word marriage with me. I cannot say I was surprised. It may not have been time to use the word before, but now it sounded right. The world needed us to be together, things just made sense this way. We would have to be married and spend the rest of our lives together. It must be so. I now began to think in ways I had not thought before. Life with her, as a couple. Where would we live, what would I do for work? All of these things were now dancing through my head as a happy, confused little song played. It was all so exciting and wonderful. I was able to forget the world and all its troubles for just a short time. Clarisse had that effect on me, and I wanted to hold on to that for as long as I could.

The next day was Sunday. Mother and father would not be as interested in attending church as I was. So, I went alone. I was sad for them not wanting to go with me. I could not understand why they would not go, but I did not push it.

I did not see too many of my friends there. Only Jeremy, who was now happily past the Clarisse issue. He had been her boyfriend before, but I don't really know if they even like each other very much. He was with his mother and younger sisters. There were about four siblings and a father missing from that picture. When I spoke to him later, he said father was tending to the sisters who were sick while his younger brother was helping. The thought never occurred to me that they were down with a bad sickness, but, when word came out that they were suffering from the Spanish Flu, it all made sense. Jimmy's passing was sad, of course. But we had no idea it could get worse somehow.

When I came home, mother asked "How was church? Had Pastor Harris asked about any of us?" She was always donating things to the church, despite never going there more than a couple days a year. She said she was a devout Christian, but proved it in her prayer and donation, as opposed to attendance.

"He did not. Church went very well, thanks!" I was now becoming a regular church-goer. I liked how it made me feel. As the sadness of the town had overtaken many, I felt much better on a daily basis when I was praying and attending regular services now. My life seemed more at peace. I could not have guessed how much I would need that peace in the coming days.

CHAPTER SEVEN

"The mailman handed this to me", said mother. Handing me a very large envelope, seemingly bigger than a regular-sized postage envelope, she stuck it in my face to show me how important it must have been. The size alone would have been enough of a suggestion. But mother's dramatic gesture made it even more pronounced.

"I am not expecting anything. Huh!" I said in a disarming way. I did not want her to worry, but it said "Selective Service" on the front, left corner. That was all I saw.

The world seemed to stand still. I could not move. It was as if I had been paralyzed. I was in fear, or something more like terror, that the envelope was about to change my life. I almost forgot what to do with it. My hands began to shake as I tore at the top of it to open it. I was too shaky to do it without tearing into the actual contents, just a bit. It was not enough to tear the paper apart, but just enough to forever make a mark on the paper that would remind me of this terrible feeling.

As I read the paper, it said I need to report to the recruiting station. It was in Reading. I needed to be there in a week. I could not read any more. It had basically knocked me down, as I looked up at mother, I realized I had sat down at some point. I did not even remember doing that.

"Well, we knew this day might come" she said. I was healthy, young, and just the kind of person who would serve his country in Europe. We were not skilled, did not have wealth, and nothing about us served us any connections to anyone important enough to get us out of this service. It seemed as though it was going to happen, and there would be nothing I could do about this.

"I will not allow you to go" declared a defiant Clarisse, with a scowl on her face that I had seldom seen. "You and I have a future together, HERE!" she exclaimed, as if I was asking her opinion if I could leave her to join the Army. I had no way of calming her.

"I cannot ignore this; it is not a request. I need to report. I just wanted you to know about it." I had actually thought I was doing her a favor by involving her in this development. Little did I realize she was not about to say thank you, as much as blame me for turning 18.

"There is no way this works for our future. You have to stay here. We are going to be married and live on a nice farm in this very village. You cannot go away now." Calming herself as she spoke, Clarisse justified her stubborn reaction with a new set of rules we were to follow, as if her alternate reality was just a choice she would make and we would all be living in that world from now on.

"How can I argue with that?" I put my hand on hers and looked into her wonderful, deep blue eyes. I noticed for the first time that when she is disturbed about something her cheeks turn a pink hue. It was like a white carnation that had just become open, hinting at a slight reddish pink in its center. I did not know I had ever noticed that part of a flower before, until now.

She was more at peace than I thought she would be with this. Maybe the touch of my hand had done it? She seemed to be more at peace than I thought possible.

"I will go to Reading with you," she stated. I guess she was making a plan to accept the situation by actually watching me go into the Selective Service office. She would be calmer now, so I could not argue that plan.

One week went by quickly. I don't think it was because I wanted that to happen, so much as the worry had overtaken me so much, I could not get past it. Everything I did that week was geared toward the trip to Reading. I did not expect to return. I was convinced I would get to the office, walk in and be fitted for a uniform right away. Not that I knew how these things worked, I was just convinced there was no chance I would be coming home again.

Father drove the wagon over the mountain as Clarisse and I talked some more. Father had heard for the first time how I was planning a future with her, and he was not surprised at all. I was happy to see he did not react to the conversation. It made me feel like we were not being foolish, but practical and upfront with our feelings.

I did not want to have more of those four months, when I was apart from Clarisse. Although, I am not sure it would have been as nice as it has been for the past month if I had not been away all that time. It was as if our separation from each other had made us somehow closer to each other. The thought had crossed my mind that I had imagined how much I actually missed her when I was away. However, now that we were together, I could not bear to imagine being apart from her again. If that had to happen, we should be fine. I was sure of that. It had to be, so we would just go on missing each other again. We would write letters and keep ourselves informed of how life would simply move along, although in a sickly way.

Father was the first to remark when he saw the church steeple, "I had forgotten how tall that building is", which actually surprised me. Of course, he had seen it before, but I foolishly assumed I was the first person in the family to see it.

"It is like the biggest steeple I have ever seen," declared Clarisse in a most innocent and sincere way. She was adorable like that. It would make me miss her more.

"When Aunt Shirley and I came over the mountain last time, we were much faster than this. Now I can enjoy the view for even longer." I savored every moment of freedom I had on that trip. The birds seemed to have learned a new song that day. It was a melody of nature that was out of a lullaby. Somewhere in the past, Brahms had gotten a great idea from something like this new tune I had heard now for the first time.

"That is the cat-bird," Father explained. He must have seen Clarisse and I looking at it as we approached the first turn on

Penn's Mountain. The bird was very plain, other than a simple, dark stripe through its head, as if it had a bad haircut.

The haircut. Not until now had I thought of that. I would be getting the typical soldier's haircut. Had I very long hair it would probably bother me more. A woman would have a much harder time with this than I would, I told myself. It's not that I could not take a shorter hair style, I just did not want to lose all of my hair. I had seen the older boys come back to town, and they hardly had any hair at all. The three boys I knew had gone with a full head of hair and came back with a nearly bald head. They rarely spoke about the haircuts. It was as if they no longer cared about the hair they used to grow on their heads. I could not imagine that change in me. While I did not really care much about the way I looked, I did not want to have this dramatic change of appearance forced upon me. All this pondering made me silent. I had not realized how much of this was in my head until we were sitting in front of the park at the top of the city.

Father asked me, again, "I said, had you seen this statue before?" He was pointing at the statue of someone at the top of the park. It was a strange statue, looked a little like a Civil War general, or something.

"Well, yes, I suppose I have. Who is it?" Oh, I knew who it was. I also knew how much my father liked to explain historical tidbits, so I acted like I had no idea.

"That is Christopher Columbus" Father explained. You know he can to the New World from Spain, but he was actually from an Italian city!" He got so very excited when he was on a roll like this. I did not have the heart to interrupt his impassioned lesson. He went on to explain what we had learned in school, so many years ago. How Columbus was venturing into an unknown world of opportunity.

I began to question if that was what was happening to me now: was I about to do the same with the Army? Was this unknown world my future?

Before I knew it, we were on Penn's Street in the heart of the downtown area. It was not as packed with people as it had been before.

"The last time I was here, we had trouble getting through the street. There were people everywhere, travelling by every mode of transportation I could imagine. It was as if they were all marching about like a bunch of ants at a picnic."

Father joined in. "Like they were trying to get into a glass jar for canning" he joked. "I've been here a few times, and it has never been this empty on a regular week-day." He seemed concerned.

We rode a bit further, turning onto 5th Street and approached the U.S. Government Building #522, home of the Selective Service Office. A very nice man opened the door for me as I approached, while Father and Clarisse rode about looking for places to leave the cart.

The whole thing took only a few minutes, which was actually a bit disappointing. The man at the desk, who wore a soldier's uniform, was intimidating, to say the least. He looked like he was all muscles, with a short, sharp haircut, and a permanent frown on his brow. No chance he was a person with whom you would want to share a long ride about town. The man was abrupt and to-the-point, not wasting any words.

"Sign this, right here, and put your initials here," he said as he pushed a paper in front of me. "Now we will call for you when we need you." Then he underwent a very brief and quick transformation. "The country will need young men like yourself, to be called upon to do your duty and keep the world safe for Democracy." He practically saluted me with that last patriotic statement.

I felt quite small in front of him, almost like an insignificant flea in front of a large, barking dog. Then, he actually did salute. I thought that odd, until I realized I was standing in front of a flag. He had saluted the flag behind me as if I was not even there. It was all so staged and practiced, which was somewhat comical. It had almost moved me to laugh out loud.

I spent a moment wondering what to do, fighting back my laughter, when I noticed the man had stood up with only one leg under him. He had been missing a leg the whole time and I did not see it until now. Had he lost a leg in the war? Was he just there, recently?

The whole tragic thing was overwhelming. I somehow grabbed at my chest in a patriotic gesture, and turned to the flag next to me. I did have much more to ask at this point, but it seemed as much a dismissive gesture by the soldier as any, so I walked out. The whole thing took only ten minutes.

When we had finished with this appointment so early into the day, yet had made this long trip, it seemed a waste of time to simply return home. So, we went to Aunt Shirley's house.

We spent the day catching up on the past month. She told me about the last baseball game she had tried to go to without me. She had gotten into a habit of going on Sundays after church, and last Sunday she tried to do that again, as the Reading team was playing at home. However, something odd happened. The game was cancelled. It was strange to have a game cancelled when there was no rain.

Father explained he heard they were worried about the spread of the Spanish Influenza, so the Sunday games were all cancelled for the future. How disappointing that must have been for so many people, especially Aunt Shirley. And, on a more confounding note, I thought the flu was basically cured. The newspapers had said this disease which was brought back from Europe had ended in Europe and was almost ended here, too. There were almost no accounts of the flu in August. This was both disappointing and confusing.

We stayed and talked for a long while, enjoying the cooler air of the late summer on her front porch. It was a nice time. Aunt Shirley really liked Clarisse, it turned out. I knew she would. The brief ride around the village a few months ago was not uncomfortable for either of them, but they did not really get to talk very much. Today, they were both able to keep my mind off of my worries, so they had a lot in common that way. Aunt Shirley could get me excited about baseball and automobile mechanics, while Clarisse would flatter me all the while, telling me how great I could be as a mechanic. Father was pretty quiet, but enjoyed seeing me happy for once in a long week.

Just before we left, Father said he had a surprise for me. While he and my mother had seemed to forget my birthday, they would make it up to me with a gift. It was more like a family gift. We went a bit further down the road, when we stopped in front of an automobile store. Somehow, when I was not aware of it, father and mother decided to buy a Model T for the family. I was going to drive it home with Clarisse in the front seat with me.

This more than made up for missing the birthday in the first place. We did have a lot going on at the time, but this was a really nice way to make up for it.

The ride home was smooth and quick. We did not wait for my father. We made it back to the village at a very quick pace. It did not give us time to talk, but we had done enough of that up to this point. It made the whole trip rather enjoyable, despite its original intent.

CHAPTER EIGHT

As the Army officer had said, the information about the draft notices would take several weeks to send to the draft board and put together a list of candidates who would then be brought in for a physical, and with all likelihood, join the U.S. Army. So, all we could do for the last few weeks of September, and into October was wait.

About three weeks had passed, and I had almost forgotten about the man who would probably be changing my life forever. He was a proud man with a sad story to tell, yet I was not in any position to hear that story. The whole thing made me feel badly for him. Although, I don't suppose he wanted to say anything to little old me, anyway.

There was a certain amount of anxiety we had all began to live with as if it was normal. Life was tenuous, and everyone would die at some point. My Father would have quoted Ben Franklin who said something about death and taxes. But it was all true. There is no way anyone can avoid it. The only problem is how soon it comes to us.

The wait made the daily activities around here rather difficult. It was like I was doing things physically with my body, but I had no idea where my mind was. Some things got done without me even realizing I had done them. The other day, for example, Father asked if I had milked the cows in the morning and I said no, because I simply did not remember doing it. But when he came back in the house about ten minutes later, he told me I must have already done it. That was pretty strange, and if I am being truthful, a little scary. How my mind was playing tricks on me!

When my mother came into the kitchen after weeding the garden, she asked if I would help her with dinner. She had a notion of some things to come, I suppose, and if I would learn more around the kitchen it might be helpful. I had helped, but may not have been…helpful. Mother had cleaned up nearly every task I started, with the exception of putting away the pots and pans after they were cleaned. That was the only task I remember doing, anyway. She said thank you for the help, but it was as I was putting away a pot that neither of us had even used. Or had we? When we ate dinner that evening, Father remarked that we had done well creating that meal, and Mother looked at me to say "thank you."

"I only put away a pot," I replied, as if Mother's look was the cue for my response. It was a little embarrassing to find out I had helped to mash the potatoes, yet had no recollection of doing so. That was odd, yet followed along with my basic thoughts for the past several days. Nothing was normal.

Honestly, I could not tell you what more I actually did for those few weeks. I know Clarisse and I had spent plenty of time together, making plans that were without any real validity. Where we would live and what our house would look like, and how many children we might have were all planned out, but I have no idea what we decided upon. These plans probably made her feel better, and certainly were a good attempt at taking my mind off of the impending draft notice.

In the early afternoons, I began to go with my mother and we would meet up with Clarisse at her mother's stand at the farmer market. For the most part, this was an effort to literally move me away from the reality that I likely faced, and waiting around at the house every day seemed like it would be all too stressful. I liked to be around Clarisse, of course, and I think Mother wanted the discussions and plans we had been making to catch the ear of Clarisse's mother. We needed to be around her family more often if we were going to "plant the seed" she would say. I am not sure what seed she meant, or what we could possibly be "planting", although I knew she was not being literal. I could not really be bothered to argue, especially since I just did not understand it. At least it took my mind off of what was coming for me.

Waiting was the worst when you did not know for what you were waiting. And then, it came. The mailman knew what we were all waiting for at our house, and he thought it best to come right up to the door and knock.

"Vell, I know vat chou people have been hoping for, and 'dis here looks like it, now." He said in a very strong a Berks County, local Pennsylvania Dutch accent. I did not know the man very well, but Father went to school with him nearby, so the accent made sense.

I was so anxious, I wanted to grab at the letter and rip it out of his hands, but at the same time, I did not even want to look at it. So, I just stood there with my mouth open. I probably had a look of shock on my face before my Mother came over and took the envelope from him.

"Thank you, very much!" She was nicer than me at this moment, and spent the next five minutes chatting away with him about his mother who was sick. I should have cared more, I know, but all I really wanted was what was in that letter.

When he left, Mother and I went back into the kitchen and sat down. She was careful not to rip anything, not really aware of the contents, nor very sure of how official anything inside the envelope might be.

I sat and looked at her with a very patient look on my face, despite my anguish. She looked calm, which must have been repressing some emotion. Was she fearful or sad? I could not tell. She handed me the letter…

"Attention Sir,

We regret to inform you that your current domestic financial situation precludes you from being enrolled in the lottery system for the draft in the United States Army at this time..."

I was a very confused by this. What had that all meant about my "economic situation"? I must have had a quizzical look on my face, because Mother immediately patted my leg and turned her head to the side, just a bit. She seemed to want to help me understand, but the words would not come out.

Mother needed a minute to consider how to phrase this. Eventually she said, "I think the one-child policy had been in effect for some time. I remember hearing about it before."

"Mother, I do not understand. Is the 'one-child policy' an explanation of my 'current domestic financial situation'?" But, as I asked it, I began to take in the big picture.

She had thought I had my heart set on being in the Army. It was not the kind of thing any of the men in my family had ever shied away from in the past. My grandfather had been in the Spanish American War and my great-grandfather served under General Meade at Gettysburg. There was even talk about a relative who was even in the Revolutionary War, although we were not sure if he had been a Hessian and escaped the prison camp near Reading, which would have meant he fought against Washington. Naturally, we did not talk about him very often.

What Mother did not realize is that I did not yearn to fight for my country. I had said some things like that a few years back, when I had turned 16. The idea then was to become an adult, and you could say all you wanted to do when you became an adult. Sometimes it sounded so foolish years later.

Since I began to go to church every Sunday, beginning with Aunt Shirley in Reading, I had other thoughts about humanity and the value of life. I could no longer even talk about taking another person's life. It just would not be acceptable. I doubt I could even think about it further, let alone plan to do so.

I was rather relieved when I heard the news. Actually, I think my mother was relieved, too. She had no idea that I would be as relieved, so when we spoke about our feelings aloud, it was rather nice to hear. We agreed that this was a good end to the whole thing.

We never spoke about the siblings I would have had when I was growing up, but they had all died young. I did not know them. They all died of illness at a young age, which had always made my mother sad. Of course I did not know them, so the only thing I knew was I could have had siblings, but I was not really sad they had passed away. However, the fact that they were not alive now, meant that I would not be serving in the Great War. It was a blessing in a way. Perhaps Mother would see it that way at some point, too.

Later in the afternoon, I went to my girlfriend's house to tell her the good news. Clarisse was overjoyed. All the waiting and now the good news to find out I would not be going away, made her cry. I was not surprised to see that, of course. I kind of expected that reaction from her. She was always getting emotional about things like that.

She told her mother, as I expected. She ran into the kitchen to exclaim that I was never going to the Army and would not leave. The way she did that, I also expected. What I did not expect was the overall reaction.

Her mother came out to give me a hug. Huh, that was odd. Nice, but odd. I don't recall ever getting a hug from Mrs. Thun before. Maybe something had changed with my relationship with her, or more appropriately, with her daughter.

The hug was warm and affectionate, like an aunt whom you haven't seen in a few years. She was not a weak woman, so the bear-style hug she threw around me was both warming and a bit more painful that I was expecting. Clarisse clearly got her strength from her mother. A hug from Clarisse was very similar. The only difference was that I usually expected those hugs. They were reserved for times when we were completely alone, and it was the appropriate amount of affection for the situation. Mrs. Thun's hug seemed forced from my end.

Or was there more to it than just her concern? Maybe she was letting me know she cared for me because I cared for her daughter? At the time, I did not foresee how that hug changed our relationship. It was evidence of her acceptance of me almost as a member of her family.

That day would prove to be much shorter than any one day in the past three weeks. That was the biggest relief of all. I think my mind was now able to focus on every individual task before me. I was no longer in a fog with every action.

I slept well that night. I had none of the dreams I had been dealing with for the past few months. That may have been the first time I was able to put the recurring dream into words. I now accepted it and all that it now had revealed to me. I knew I had been scared, but now it made much more sense. Furthermore, my relationships were now becoming far more clear to me.

CHAPTER NINE

"Jump!" I yelled, as Clarisse clutched the exterior brick walls of the second floor of the First Trust Bank of Reading. She had little chance to make it out alive if she went back inside the window.

The bank was three stories tall and mostly stone and brick construction. A fire that would burn down this place could only be a very hot one. It would be very destructive, and I could not help to put that out.

Started on the first floor, it consumed all the paper and many of the wood furniture pieces as it ripped through everything in its way. Somehow, Clarisse made it up the steps to the office space above, where she was now trapped.

I had been away, and only hearing the sirens within the past few seconds, had little chance to make it to the building on time to do anything but watch in horror, as she perched herself up there, waiting for someone to get a ladder up to her. But there seemed to be no time.

I raced around looking for something that might help to reach her, but nothing was there. If only I had been around to help when the fire started, or maybe I could have gone into the bank with her, instead of…where had I been?

Looking down, I hardly recognized my body. On my chest was a medal and a ribbon. Where that came from or for what purpose, it would not be revealed. I guess I had won them for something, but I am not completely sure. My pants legs flared out a little, and were then tucked into a very odd-looking pair of socks, which were tucked into army boots.

This was my uniform after having fought in the Great War, and I was away for too long. I could not take care of…wait… Clarisse was not alone on that ledge…

"Help us, help us!" cried Aunt Shirley. Mother stood next to her, as well. Suddenly, the ladder was at the scene. I grabbed at it, only to realize it was broken. No, it would not work to help them. I could do nothing but watch as they were consumed by the fire.

And then I awoke. Thank goodness. What a horrible dream. Serving in the army would not likely have such an effect on my life, nor on those I love. But, I was clearly worried about them.

Wait, those I love included my mother, which was obvious, Aunt Shirley, which also made a lot of sense, and Clarisse. Well, that was interesting. I had not realized that had happened.

As I explained the sequence of events to Clarisse, she looked horrified. This dream had not been a sign of things to come, or even things that I worried about openly. It was symbolic of my inability to help and be there, had I been off to war winning medals. Or, something like that.

She seemed to grasp that concept, yet still felt horror at the imagery of her, my mother and my aunt perishing in a fire right before my eyes. She was in tears at the very thought of it. When she realized I had been seeing this in my sleep for the past month, she felt terribly for me, and wept openly in front of me. Now that was not an altogether unusual occurrence, it was still something that was worthy of note.

When I finally completed that last part, revealing my feelings and how I had put her in the same grouping as the women I loved, she stopped crying. Although, it was only for a moment. She tilted her head the way one might when you try to understand someone in a different language. I always assumed it was for a better hearing position, but in this case, she heard me just fine.

She actually stood up. We were sitting on a swing that hung from the big oak tree in her back yard. They had rows of trees, which mostly grew fruit, but this one was reserved for our big, long conversations. We often disappeared back there for hours when we wanted to be alone. It was a perfect place to be away from all other people. The swing was nice, but she only swung on it for the first few minutes, before we just stopped moving it, altogether. And then, unexpectedly, she practically jumped up.

"What, exactly are you saying?" She had to make me clarify.

"I suppose what I am saying is…What I mean to say is…" I must have sounded completely stupid to her. As if I could not put a sentence together.

"You do not really know what you are saying, do you?" she giggled.

"I am saying I love you," I blurted out. The words hung there in the air and slowly drifted around like the leaves that were falling from the trees around us. I was accused of not being very romantic in the past, but I waited to tell her about my dreams until the most beautiful day possible, and in the most beautiful place I could imagine.

Maybe the dream should not have been the way I started this conversation, because she looked even more confused. Maybe I was not as good at this stuff as I had first thought. And, maybe she was right about me that way. She reached out and kissed me. I got it right. Or, at least close enough.

Mrs. Thun was overjoyed to hear about my intentions to marry Clarisse. After all, as mother had said, I had "planted the seed" earlier with spending so much time around them.

We had plans to make and things to do, so we began in earnest to make those plans. First, we wanted to go to the church and speak to the minister about a wedding. The spring was the best time with weather concerns in the winter, and we wanted people to come from outside the village, with sat in a valley, so the weather had to be nice enough to do that.

"Let's tell the minister we want an April wedding," Clarisse declared as she motioned to the trees which had lost most of their leaves by now.

"I suppose that would be fine" I replied, having not given much thought to it, other than I wanted to start my life with her as soon as possible.

And we enjoyed the walk to the church for about five more minutes when we noticed something strange in the church parking lot. The minister's new automobile was not there. He had planned this meeting time every week, and it was not altogether unusual to see him at the church every day, let alone a Saturday afternoon. But he was not here now.

We knocked on the door to the office behind the church and nobody came around. While a strange occurrence, it was not alarming. We walked back home, supposing nothing bad had happened. We were sadly mistaken.

"You did not actually come into contact with anyone over there, did you?" asked my mother in an altogether accusatory tone.

"Umm, no ma'am, we did not!" I was surprised the word 'ma'am' came out of my mouth. Perhaps that was the appropriate reaction of a young man when his mother chastised him for some wrongdoing, but was this such a time? "Why do you ask?"

"The minister was taken away to the hospital yesterday" said mother. Not something anyone had expected to hear.

"But what is wrong?" asked Clarisse with a grave concern. "Surely he is not sick?"

No one had any idea what he had been doing for the past week, other than interacting with many of the people of the village. But that had been enough to send him to the hospital in Reading. That was not even the first place one would go to recover from the Spanish Influenza, so we had not thought that was going through the village. At least at first.

Soon, it became apparent that was exactly what was going through the village. It spread quicker than anyone had anticipated, and faster than anyone had seen before.

Almost all my friends from school had now been sick except for me and Clarisse. The scary thing was that we had just seen most of them the past few days when we went around telling them we wanted to be wed.

This flu seemed to be hitting young people hard, and sending all kinds of folks to their beds, and some to even the hospital. I wondered how this could have been the same disease my parents had, but most people seemed to think that was exactly what it was.

We were told the illness was licked. Sunday baseball games and larger gatherings were banned, but that seemed like a pretty ridiculous overreaction to something the newspaper even declared "finished in Berks County, and perhaps the country, altogether". We rejoiced at the news when we had read it, but now those very words seemed like a lie.

So many people would be sick and suffering over the next few weeks, and the village looked empty and rather different. I was really nervous walking around the village, from the market, to the church, to Clarisse's house. It was not the same at home, knowing my parents had the disease already. But the nerves were again as fraught as when I thought the army was going to take me away.

The days were getting much shorter now, and the wedding planning seemed to be filled with angst. We talked about a house, a job, all kinds of things, but never anything without a discussion of the illness. We began to worry if the whole world was going to get sick.

The newspaper read, "Death Toll Reaches 2,000" for the month of October. There was little chance we were going to have another day without fear of this disease again.

CHAPTER TEN

At first, the situation was oddly sedate, as a pleasant breeze blew through the otherwise humid late October afternoon in the valley. Our village was situated close enough to the ocean to receive moist air in the summer, yet far enough that it seemed too difficult to travel there in a day. I had some friends who went to the Atlantic coast, but they had since moved away from the village. Now, it just seemed like the most unpleasant moisture in the air, and it was not even summer anymore.

The death toll seemed like an otherworldly phenomenon to us. Clarisse and I had found a flower we wanted to be on her dress for the wedding. I don't know what it was, exactly, but it was pink. Her plans were my plans, although I do not think much of it was my original idea. Although we continued to make plans, we could not shake the talk about the deadly reality in which we now found ourselves.

We had heard about the deaths in the United States, Pennsylvania, Reading, and even Berks County on the whole, but we never thought about it much in the village. Of course, while Jimmy Granite's unfortunate death, while months ago, was a part of this disease and its horrific statistics, it seemed like another illness entirely back in March. Now it was nearly November, and we had no idea if these new cases were really a part of the Jimmy Granite illness. Many people thought it was a different thing, entirely. Regardless, the flu was killing people all over the county, and we were in the middle of it.

On an average day, the people of our village were out and about, travelling on the roads by foot, horse-drawn wagon, or the now-affordable automobile. It was busy around here in the summer, autumn, and even in the winter. Yet, this October it was looking rather deserted. There were normally people in the farmers' market, but today there was no one. Not a single person for this late season was shopping here. The market, itself was only at about half the regular vendors. I could not believe my eyes. This was a time when people had been buying apples, green peppers, cucumbers, and all kinds of late-season vegetables, and you had to get there early to get your favorite picks. Yet, today you could have found the market loaded with quite the choice of fruits and vegetables. It was almost as if the farmers had to be ready to let their foods rot in their stalls.

The sense of awe as we left the market was hovering around us while we got onto the main street. We went a block-and-a-half before we saw another person. The normal rush hour of our late mornings around here did not even resemble what were seeing now. I wondered how the fear of a virus could seemingly shut down the whole town.

This was getting eerie. Clarisse recalled passing by the school yesterday, and seeing five children waiting in front for the door to open. On a normal day, the classes all lined up out front before the school was opened. Regardless of the weather or time of year, there was always at least 30 students standing in front of the school. But she saw five. I thought she was exaggerating at first. Now, I believed everything she said about it. This place was looking more like a ghost town.

Most people of the village were just sitting in their homes, hunkering down and waiting out the disease. We had moved on from the old, traditional beliefs that being in the country meant you would be relatively healthy in your environment, and you might not ever get sick. Now, we understood that something like this flu was passed by humans, and through human contact. The fear of seeing another human seemed to be taking hold now. It felt like a fear that was growing and creeping into our town's every day activities. Almost paralyzing our very existence.

As we finally met with the minister from the neighboring town, the plans were well under way. We took the Model T, as my parents did not seem to want to drive it all that often. In addition, they really did not know how to fix it if anything went wrong. I had gotten quite good at the fixing part, and they were rather impressed. Furthermore, my parents really did not have anywhere to go most of the time. Father was far more comfortable in his wagon, and Mother preferred to walk.

Clarisse and I began our trip home, yet as we left the parking lot we came upon a man in the parking lot. I was not sure of where he came from, exactly, but he was in front of the car without warning. We slammed on the brakes of the car, just in time, as the man began to shout at us. The whole thing was jarring, both physically and emotionally. Yet Clarisse seemed to really be rattled by it. The man just walked away as though nothing had happened, once I leaned out and apologized. I believe it was his fault, since there were really not too many automobiles around town, and he clearly did not think to look around him before he stepped in front of the Model T.

Perhaps it was the nervous nature of that encounter, or maybe the emotional nature of our wedding that we were in the middle of planning, but as soon as we arrived at her house, Clarisse broke into tears. I could not hide my surprise about the whole thing. When her mother came running out, I was afraid her first thought would have been that I had caused this outpouring of emotion. But that was not so. In fact, it was almost the opposite, as I would later come to find out. She was hiding something from me and she was crying as a result. I had only remotely guessed her mother was in on it, as she seemed to console Clarisse, and then, oddly me. It was all so unusual, that I just sat there with a very dumb look on my face. When Clarisse came back around to her normal self, she actually chuckled at my appearance. I must have looked pretty confused.

Her mother began, "you kids have obviously had a long day, why don't you both come in for supper."

I was still a bit confused, but was perfectly willing to accept the invitation to the famous food that her mother was always cooking. She was quite the chef, actually. However, Clarisse had other ideas.

Utterly confounding me, she said, "no, thanks, he should be getting back to his parents now." I almost sulked away wondering if I had done something wrong.

Mother and father were in the kitchen waiting for me when I got home. That was never a good sign.

The fear that had swept through town had not crept into our house. Mostly because my parents had already had the disease, but also because my parents were fairly level-headed about most things. A disease, commonly called a pandemic at this level, was not the kind of thing to rattle them.

But today seemed different. As I sat down with them, I could sense a deep concern. The placid look on their faces from this morning had given way, now something quite menacing seem to be behind their looks of fear. They were concerned for me, I suppose.

"Son, we need to talk," said Father. He was really one to get right into it. Whatever the point was, he would be the one to make it.

"Clarisse and I have spoken to the minister and we are ready for the wedding. It will be in--" I was cut off.

"Not that." He continued, "It's your Aunt Shirley...Son, she has contracted the Spanish Influenza. Apparently, Reading has been hit very hard with this illness and it has wiped the place out."

I did not know where to look. Father was stern and serious. The underlying concern was clear now. Mother was sad, and it was now obvious she had been crying.

"What is our plan here? Are we going to go to her and take care of her?" After all, she was there for me when my parents were ill. It just seemed obvious that we would be there for her, now.

"We cannot go there. The doctors have sent her to the hospital. It is pretty bad." Father finished speaking. There was just nothing more to say.

CHAPTER ELEVEN

Aunt Shirley lived in a very wealthy part of the city. Center Avenue, or Centre if you used the older style, was a very wealthy part of town. We often talked about all the wonderful homes there, and that she was rather lucky to live there. I was happy for her to have that place. It was what she and her husband wanted from the beginning. They had money, most likely from his family, and had apparently liked the lifestyle of that part of town. It was quite lovely.

Any time a person who lived in that part of town became sick, the high society of Reading all had talked about it. They talked about a good deal of things, mostly things that were considered gossip around here.

In the village, if one had talked about another neighbor, it became known very quickly who had talked about whom. It could get pretty embarrassing if word got out that you had spread a rumor, which kept things pretty quiet. At least, that was the way I saw it.

Aunt Shirley's neighbors were quick to spot her unattended milk bottles on the front porch, and the daily newspaper all rolled up. They knocked on her door by dinner time. When she failed to come to the door, the neighbors had rushed to the police, as well as the doctor to ask for help. Thank goodness they did that, as it seemed to have affected her very quickly.

The feeling around town had been much the same as the feeling around the village. People were now reacting in ways we have never seen. We saw businesses abandoned. Folks who regularly went to work every day, seemed to just be staying home now.

Newspapers were now filled with signs of war and disease, and little else. Nothing was going on in the world outside of those two things. The world in 1918 was quite simple. You would either die in the war in Europe, or stay in your home to avoid the disease. There was no other way to survive.

Fear had taken over. The world had reacted in such a way that everything seemed to stand still. Schools were cancelled, churches were closed and businesses shuttered. The disease they said was gone here was now winning. We had no end in sight.

When we arrived in Reading, Clarisse and I saw right away that Aunt Shirley's house needed a soft touch, plants inside needed to be watered, which Clarisse immediately did. I went around to the back door and checked on the property. It needed some serious tending.

As we moved about in various tasks all day long, it was a bit of a surprise that the day had passed and darkness had fallen. It was too late to return to the village, but the job had to be done, so we stayed the night in the house. It felt warm and cozy. We both thought it felt strange staying in a house before we were married, but there was little choice. All that work needed to be done, and Aunt Shirley had no way of tending to any of it from the hospital. She would be gone for a longer time than we realized.

The night went fast. We awoke at a later hour than we were used to, and it rattled me a bit when I awoke to find I was not at my parents' home. I felt oddly as if it was spring again and I was staying with my aunt while my parents were sick, when it was quite the reverse this time.

We had a nice breakfast which Clarisse fixed. I had no idea she had the ability to make such a nice meal. The fact that we had never had breakfast together before had eluded me until now. She was actually prepared for it, and was ready with a big smile when I walked into the kitchen. It was a bit like we were play acting the roles of a married couple. Something about it felt so right, yet the circumstances were not what we wanted.

We tidied up a bit more and then got on the road back to the village. Having spent as little time in Reading as possible, I noted the trip to the hospital would have been an extra few minutes. But we were expected back, so we did not delay.

About two weeks later, we were told the bad news. It was as bad as I had ever had. Aunt Shirley would not be coming back to her house.

All I could do was hope she was now with her husband somewhere, happy. There was little anyone could say to me, or mother, who was also taking it pretty hard. Clarisse had even given me space to grieve, without the usual attention to try to cheer me. She was so good at making me happy, that this was unusual. But I really needed some time to just feel upset.

Mother made the worst dinner that evening. It was a true sign that her heart was not into it. She was a good cook, and this was not her best effort. She was upset, but insisted she make dinner. We thought it would take her mind off of everything. It worked for a time. Then we had to eat, and emotions came flooding back to her. The dinner was not so bad it would have made one want to cry, but she did. Father and I knew it could not be the dinner.

We spoke no further about it for the rest of the day. Instead, mother had gone about making plans for the church in Reading. It was a special place, one which I often enjoyed going to during my time there. It would be a moving service, I was certain.

Father said he was sure Aunt Shirley had thought of me when she passed. I did not know how he could have known that. But, as her only nephew, and with no children, I suppose it could have been true.

CHAPTER TWELVE - EPILOGUE

The service was simple. The minister spoke in his usual tone for a typical Sunday service. He greeted all the parishioners, and thanked us for coming. We spoke to the few around us and went on our way back to the house.

We drove in to our house on Center Avenue in Reading, just in time to have the neighbors pass by on their daily walk. Friendly folks, actually. Clarisse gave them a wave, and engaged in very usual, courteous conversation. She had obviously made a reference to her belly, and rubbed her hand over the baby. She was not "showing" yet, but it was clear that is where the conversation would have led. She could not stop talking about the baby since she found out a month ago.

Our wedding was wonderful. We danced more than I ever thought I could. I thought I did not know how to dance, but all the practice we had certainly made up for it. The music, the food, the guests, and everything was so memorable.

Life had returned to normal in Reading. The flu seemed to be in the past now. Father and Mother wrote to us about the village being full of people again. Clarisse's mother, or "mom" as she wanted me to call her, had also written that her stand at the farmer's market was doing well again. She, and my parents were very happy for us. No one back in the village seemed to be any worse off than before the virus, with the exceptions of the few folks who had passed away. Jimmy Granite, of course, would forever be missed. It was becoming less common to hear of anyone getting sick these past few months. It all seemed behind us.

The war in Europe was over. We had no idea for how much longer the peace conference would last, but all the signs seemed to point the war being over for good. The peace seemed to matter much less than the actual end of fighting, as so many had died by late March of 1919.

My birthday was two days ago. Clarisse and I celebrated at our "new" home on Center Avenue in Reading. It was just the two of us. It would be that way for a few more months, at least.

As we entered our house, I thought of Aunt Shirley. She wanted us to live here in Reading at her house. Father was right, she had thought of me when she left the house and all its belongings to me and Clarisse. It would always be in my thoughts when the house got a little too quiet. I imagined when the children got a little older, that would not happen too often.

Tomorrow I would start my job as an automobile mechanic. Not that I could have thanked her for this, but it was Aunt Shirley's idea to put me on this path. I did not realize how much I enjoyed working on automobiles. If not for her, I would not have considered this as a potential career. I may have just stayed in the valley, tending to the cows in a daily routine of milking and tending to their needs. There would have been nothing wrong with that, of course. It was just what I would have been expected to do. It would have been something that my grandfather and probably great-grandfather would have done. It was what was expected of me because no one thought any different.

Aunt Shirley was not the kind of person who wanted me to do what was expected just because that was what we had always done. She wanted me to be happy. She wanted me to have the life I wanted. I would live in a way that she would be proud. I can be a mechanic and live in a nice home in Reading, in the city, because it is what makes me happy. Life will go on the way that she would have wanted it to. I will live my life in the way that she would want, and in a way that I am most happy.

Father wanted me to come here, he said he did not want me to be tied to the farm like some indentured servant. He began a history lesson as he explained it, but I don't remember much beyond that.

Mother may not have wanted me to leave the village...ever. I am not sure what we would have done there, maybe live with my parents? Maybe live with Clarisse's mother. I do not know. It was another lifetime ago that we would even have considered a life like that for us. Mother would be happy for us, where ever we were, she would just have preferred that be nearer to her. I would probably understand that better when I have my own children.

In my new job, I will be helping people. The industry in which I chose to work would be a new and exciting one. People would be constantly learning new things about these cars and making new models all the time. In fact, as we modernize, I will continue to learn and improve myself. I rather enjoy the education. I never knew I would so appreciate the push I would be getting toward continuously making myself better. This new job would require that, and I felt ready for the challenge. I think I will be pretty good at it.

As we sat out on the front porch, Clarisse and I thought about the past year, and how difficult it had been in so many ways. We saw many family and friends suffer, some in the most extreme ways possible. Disease and death were always certain, but this past year seemed to bring that to us more than we could have expected. We saw a war hit its peak for our soldiers, killing many and making our country suffer for it. It would not be a year we would ever want to repeat any time soon.

In the end, as we reflect back on the year, we realize how lucky Clarisse and I actually were to be where we are today. We owe a lot to our parents, and especially Aunt Shirley. While everything worked out fine for us, we were happy to be past 1918. We hoped nothing would ever happen like this to us again.